WELL LOVED TALES

The Wizard of Oz

by L F BAUM
retold by JOAN COLLINS
illustrated by ANGUS McBRIDE

Ladybird Books

THE GREAT WHIRLWIND

Dorothy was an orphan. She lived in America, in the middle of the great Kansas prairie, with her Uncle Henry, who was a farmer, and Aunt Em, his wife. Their house was small, with only one room, and a trapdoor in the floor, leading to a cellar. This was because there were often whirlwinds on the prairie, that crushed any buildings in their path. When they came, the family went down into the cellar, and were safe.

When Dorothy looked out, she saw nothing but the great grey prairie. There were no trees, and the earth was cracked by the sun.

Even Aunt Em and Uncle Henry looked grey. They worked hard, and never smiled.

Dorothy did not look grey! She laughed, and played with her little black dog, Toto. Dorothy loved him dearly.

One day the sky grew very dark. Uncle Henry looked worried. Dorothy picked up Toto. Aunt Em was washing the dishes.

They heard the low wail of the wind, and saw the grass rippling and bending.

"There's a whirlwind coming, Em!" cried Uncle Henry, and ran to look after the cows.

"Quick, Dorothy!" Aunt Em screamed. "Run for the cellar!" She opened the trapdoor and scuttled down the ladder.

Just as Dorothy grabbed Toto, the wind caught the house, and she fell headlong on the floor. The house whirled round two or three times and rose slowly in the air.

Dorothy felt as if she were going up in a balloon. The whirlwind had sucked the house up and carried it away like a feather.

Toto nearly fell through the trapdoor, but Dorothy grabbed him by his ears and closed it. Then she crawled over to her bed and lay down.

Hours went by, and Dorothy got over her fright. In spite of the swaying of the house, and the wailing of the wind, she fell asleep.

DOROTHY MEETS THE MUNCHKINS

Dorothy was awakened by a sudden bump. The house had stopped moving! She ran to the door to see where they were.

The whirlwind had set them down gently in a beautiful country. There were fruit trees, flowers and singing birds. It was quite different from Kansas.

As Dorothy gazed she saw a group of queer little people coming towards her. There were three men, wearing high boots and dressed in blue, and a little old woman, dressed in white. They all wore round hats that went up to a high point.

They came up to Dorothy, and the little woman cried: "Welcome to the Land of the Munchkins! We are grateful to you for killing the Wicked Witch of the East, who has made us work as her slaves for so long!"

Dorothy was very puzzled. She knew she had never killed anybody.

The Munchkins took her up to the house, and showed her two silver slippers, poking out at one corner. The whirlwind had dropped the house on top of the Wicked Witch and squashed her!

"That is the end of her!" said the little woman. "Those are her magic slippers. You must have them."

"Who are you?" asked Dorothy.

"I am the Good Witch of the North, come to help the Munchkins. My sister is the Good Witch of the South. We were not strong enough on our own to get rid of the Wicked Witches of the East and West. But, thanks to you, this one is gone!"

"Who are the Munchkins?"

"They live in the eastern part of the Land of Oz. The Quadlings live in the South, the Winkies in the West, and the North is my home. In the centre is the Emerald City, where the Wizard of Oz lives."

"I thought all the Witches and Wizards had died long ago!" said Dorothy.

"Not the ones in the Land of Oz," replied the Witch. Dorothy told her new friends about Uncle Henry and Aunt Em, and asked them the way back to Kansas.

"The Land of Oz is surrounded by a desert which is very dangerous to cross," said the Munchkins.

Dorothy began to cry, and the Munchkins pulled out their hankies too, in sympathy.

The Good Witch looked thoughtful. "You must go to the Emerald City!" she said. "The Wizard of Oz will help you!"

"How do I get there?" asked Dorothy.

"You must walk there," said the Witch. "Along the Yellow Brick Road."

"Can't you come too?"

"No, but I will give you a magic kiss to protect you!" The Good Witch kissed Dorothy on the forehead and left a shiny mark. Then she whirled round on her left heel three times, and disappeared.

HOW DOROTHY SAVED THE SCARECROW

Dorothy gave Toto and herself some breakfast. She put on a clean blue and white checked dress, and her pink sunbonnet.

Her shoes were nearly worn out, so she put on the Wicked Witch's silver slippers. Then, with a loaf of bread in a basket, she and Toto set off to find the Yellow Brick Road.

The countryside was pretty, with neat blue fences and fields of ripe yellow corn. The Munchkins came out of their round blue houses to greet her.

"How far is it to the Emerald City?" she asked.

"It is as well to keep away from Oz," they said, shaking their heads. "It is a long way to the City."

But Dorothy bravely decided not to turn back. When she had gone several miles, she climbed on to a fence to sit and rest, near a big cornfield.

In the field was a Scarecrow, perched high on a pole. His head was a small sack stuffed with straw, with eyes, nose and mouth painted on it. He wore an old blue pointed hat, a faded blue suit stuffed with straw, and old boots with blue tops.

As Dorothy looked at the painted face, one of the Scarecrow's eyes closed in a wink, and he nodded in a friendly way. Dorothy climbed down and went over to him.

"Can you talk?" she asked.

"Of course I can! How do you do?"

"Quite well," said Dorothy politely. "How do you do?"

"Not very well," said the Scarecrow. "It's boring being stuck up on this pole all day to scare the crows."

"I'll lift you down," said Dorothy. He was quite light, because he was stuffed with straw.

The Scarecrow asked who she was and where she was going. When Dorothy told him she was going to the Emerald City to ask the Wizard to send her back to Kansas, he asked if he could come too. "Perhaps the Wizard might give me some brains. You see, I have none, as my head is full of straw!"

Dorothy said that he could come, and they walked back to the road. The Scarecrow carried her basket.

THE RESCUE OF THE TIN WOODMAN

The travellers found an empty cottage to spend the night in. The Scarecrow did not eat breakfast, because his mouth was only painted on, and he never slept at night.

"It must be a nuisance to have to sleep and eat and drink!" he said. "But it must be worth the bother, to have brains!"

By this time they had walked into a forest. Suddenly, between the trees, Dorothy saw something shining in the sunlight.

One of the trees was partly chopped through. Standing beside it, with an axe lifted in his hands, was a man made entirely of tin.

As they looked, he gave a deep groan.

"Can we help you?" cried Dorothy.

"I can't move because my joints are rusted," he said. "Could you fetch the oil-can from my cottage? If I am oiled, I shall be able to move again."

Dorothy quickly fetched the oil-can. She and the Scarecrow helped him to move so that he was able to put down the axe.

He thanked them, and when he heard where they were going, he said, "Do you suppose the Wizard would give me a heart?" He explained that the Wicked Witch of the East had turned him into tin and taken his heart away. He wanted it back, so that he could have feelings like other people.

Dorothy agreed, so the Tin Woodman shouldered his axe, and they all went on through the forest, along the Yellow Brick Road.

THE COWARDLY LION

Every so often, they could hear a deep growl from some wild animals hiding among the trees.

"Don't be afraid," said the Tin Woodman to Dorothy. "I have my axe, and you have the mark of the Good Witch on your forehead."

Just then a terrible roar was heard, and a great tawny lion bounded on to the road. With a blow of his paw he knocked the Scarecrow over. He struck at the Tin Woodman, but his claws only scratched the tin.

Toto ran up to him barking, and the Lion opened his jaws to bite him. Dorothy rushed forward and slapped the great beast smartly on his nose.

"You coward!" she said. "Fancy a big animal like you trying to bite such a little dog! And you knocked over the poor Scarecrow!"

"I'm sorry!" said the Lion, rubbing his nose with his paw. "I can't help it! Everyone expects a Lion to be brave, so I just roar and pounce at people and they run away. But really I am very frightened myself!"

"If you had no heart, like me, you might not be such a coward," said the Tin Woodman. "But I am going to the great Wizard to ask him for a heart!"

"And I'm going to ask him for some brains!" chimed in the Scarecrow.

"I think I'll go with you. He might give me some courage."

"Yes, and you can keep the other wild beasts away from us," said Dorothy.

So off they went, and before long, they were all good friends.

THE JOURNEY TO SEE THE WIZARD

That night the Tin Woodman chopped some wood and built them a fire.

In the morning, they found they had to cross a wide deep ditch with jagged rocks at the bottom.

"I think I could jump over it," said the Lion, rather doubtfully. "I'm terribly afraid of falling, but I suppose it has to be done."

So the Scarecrow, who was the lightest, sat on the Lion's back, as he crouched at the edge of the precipice. Then he gave a great spring and landed on the other side. They all cheered, so he went back and fetched the others, one at a time.

They hurried on, until they came to another deep ditch. This time it was too wide for the Lion to jump.

"I know!" said the Scarecrow. "If the Tin Woodman cuts down that tree, it will fall across the ditch and we can walk over!"

"What a good idea!" said the Lion. "One would almost think you had brains in your head, instead of straw!"

They did as the Scarecrow suggested, and soon they were out of the forest, on the banks of a river, in lovely countryside.

"How are we going to cross?" said the Scarecrow. "I can't swim!"

"Nor can I," said the Tin Woodman. "But I can make a raft!"

21

OVER THE RIVER

When they had crossed the river on the Tin Woodman's raft, they found themselves in the country again.

There were green fields, green fences and green houses on either side of the road. The people were dressed just like the Munchkins, only in green instead of blue.

"This must be the Land of Oz!" said Dorothy.

But the people were not very friendly. "The Wizard will not see you!" they said. "He never comes out of the palace."

"What does he look like?" asked Dorothy.

"None of us has ever seen him. He can change his shape, because he is a magician!"

THE GUARDIAN OF THE GATE

The friends went on down the Yellow Brick Road, till at last they saw a beautiful green glow in the sky.

"That must be the Emerald City!" cried Dorothy.

And, sure enough, the green glow grew brighter and brighter, till they came to a high, thick, bright green wall.

The Yellow Brick Road ended there in front of a big gate, studded with emeralds, so bright that even the Scarecrow had to blink his painted eyes.

They rang the bell, and the gate opened, letting them into a high arched room, glittering with emeralds.

There sat a little green man, with a large green box by his side. "I am the Guardian of the Gate!" he said. "What do you want in the Emerald City?"

"We've come to see the Wizard!" said Dorothy.

"I hope you have a good reason," said the Guardian. "The Wizard is so terrible, he will destroy you instantly, if you haven't. I will take you to the Palace, but you must all wear these green spectacles. The brightness of the Emerald City will blind you if you don't!" And the Guardian opened the box, which was full of pairs of glasses.

So they each put on a pair of spectacles, and followed the Guardian into the City.

THE WONDERFUL EMERALD CITY OF OZ

Even with the spectacles on, Dorothy and her friends were dazzled by the splendour of the green marble City, studded with emeralds. The sky was green, and even the people, who stared at the strangers, looked green. The stalls in the market sold green candy and even green lemonade!

The Palace of Oz was guarded by a soldier with a long green beard, who went to tell the

Wizard that they had arrived. While they waited, Dorothy had to put on a green dress because she was going to see the Wizard.

When the soldier came back, he explained that the Wizard would see them one at a time, Dorothy first. "Because you have the mark of the Good Witch on your forehead. And you are wearing silver slippers and a green dress!"

Dorothy was taken to the door of the Throne Room. A bell rang as a signal for her to go in.

The Throne Room was splendid. It had a high
arched roof, sparkling with emeralds, and a big
light, as bright as the sun, in the ceiling. A great
green marble throne stood in the centre.

On the seat was an enormous Bald Head with no body, arms or legs. The eyes rolled about, and Dorothy heard a squeaky voice say: "I am the Great and Terrible Wizard! Who are you and why have you come?"

"I am Dorothy, the Meek and Humble. I have come to ask you to send me back to Uncle Henry and Aunt Em in Kansas."

"Where did you get your silver shoes?"

Dorothy told him about the Wicked Witch of the East. "And where did you get the mark on your forehead?" he asked.

And Dorothy told him about the Good Witch of the North.

"You must do something for me if you want to go back to Kansas! Kill the Wicked Witch of the West!"

"I can't! I'm only a little girl!" Dorothy protested.

"You killed the Witch of the East!" said the voice sternly.

"But that was an accident!" said Dorothy tearfully. She went back, very upset, to tell her friends what the Wizard had said she must do.

DOROTHY'S FRIENDS SEE THE WIZARD

The next day, the Scarecrow was sent for.

This time, the Wizard took the shape of a beautiful Green Lady with a jewelled crown and wings like a butterfly.

The Scarecrow asked for brains, but he got the same answer as Dorothy. He would have to kill the Witch of the West first.

Then the Tin Woodman had his turn. This time the Wizard was a terrible Beast, covered with woolly green hair. He was the size of an elephant, and had a head like a rhinoceros. But, as the Tin Woodman had no heart, he was not frightened.

He got the same answer as the others. He had to help Dorothy to kill the Witch of the West, before he got his heart.

Finally the Lion came. This time the Wizard was a Ball of Fire, which burned the Lion's whiskers.

"Bring me proof that the Wicked Witch is dead, and I will give you courage," said the voice of the Ball.

The Lion went back to the others. "We shall have to do as he says, or I shall never get my courage!"

"Nor I my brains!" said the Scarecrow.

"Nor I my heart!" said the Tin Woodman.

"And I shall never go back to Kansas!" said Dorothy.

THE SEARCH FOR THE WICKED WITCH

The soldier directed them.

"Keep going to the West, where the sun sets. But be careful. Once the Witch knows you are in her land, she will make you her slaves."

The Wicked Witch of the West had only one eye, but that was like a powerful telescope. She sat at the door of her castle and looked all around her country, till she saw Dorothy and her friends sleeping, a long way away.

So she blew a silver whistle and called up a pack of bloodthirsty wolves. "Go to those people and tear them to pieces!" she ordered.

"Very well," growled the leader of the pack and dashed away, followed by the others, snarling.

But the Tin Woodman was awake. He seized his axe. As the wolves came on, showing their bright teeth, he cut off all their heads one by one!

The Witch was so angry, she blew her whistle and summoned a flock of ugly black crows. "Peck their eyes out and tear them to pieces!" she screamed. The crows flew off, cackling.

But the Scarecrow spread out his arms. The crows flew past him one by one, and he caught each one in turn, and twisted its neck.

Then the Wicked Witch sent for a swarm of fierce black bees. "Sting them to death!" she ordered.

But the bees broke off all their stings when they attacked the Tin Woodman, and that was the end of them!

The Witch was furious! In her cupboard was a Golden Cap. Whoever owned it could call three times on the Winged Monkeys who would obey any order they were given. She had used it twice already, so this was the last time.

She read out a secret spell written inside the brim.

The sky grew dark. Then there was a rushing of wings. The sun came out and the sky was full of great monkeys, with wings on their shoulders. The largest of all, the King of the Monkeys, swooped down to the Witch.

"You have called us for the third and last time! What do you want?"

"Destroy Dorothy and her friends, all except that Lion! I want him for a slave."

Off went the Monkeys. They seized the Tin Woodman and dropped his body on the rocks, so that it broke into bits. They pulled all the straw out of the Scarecrow, and threw his clothes into a tree. They tied the Lion up and took him to the castle, where he was shut up in an iron cage.

But they could not harm Dorothy, because of

the Good Witch's mark. So they took her to the castle, where the Wicked Witch gave her a bucket and scrubbing brush, and made her clean the stone floors. Poor Dorothy!

The Lion would not work, so the Witch starved him. She knew Dorothy's slippers were magic, so she tried to steal them, kicking Toto out of the way!

But that made Dorothy so angry, she took her bucket of water and flung it all over the Witch!

To her surprise the Witch began to shrink and melt away!

"Oh dear! What have I done?" cried Dorothy.

"Didn't you know that water would be the death of me?" croaked the Witch, and melted into a shapeless mass on the floor.

Tidy Dorothy cleaned it up and ran to set the Lion free.

When the Winkies knew the Witch was dead and they were no longer slaves, they repaired the Tin Woodman as good as new, and stuffed the straw back into the Scarecrow's clothes.

Then Dorothy read out the secret spell inside the Golden Cap, and asked the Winged Monkeys to take them all back to the City of Oz.

THE RETURN TO THE EMERALD CITY

When they arrived, the friends made their way to the Throne Room, but it was empty! Only a squeaky voice came down from the ceiling. "I am invisible to mortal eyes!" it said. "What have you come for?"

"For you to keep your promises, now we have killed the Wicked Witch!"

"I'll have to think about that! Come back tomorrow!" said the voice.

At that, the Lion gave an angry roar. Toto jumped away from him, and knocked over a screen that stood in the corner.

Behind it, there crouched a queer-looking little bald old man with a wrinkled face.

"Who are you?" asked the Scarecrow.

"I am the Great and Terrible Wizard! Please don't hurt me!" the little man whimpered.

"So you're *not* a Beast, *nor* a Lady, *nor* a Ball of Fire! What are you?" asked the Tin Woodman.

"I'm a Humbug!" squeaked the Wizard. "I'm just an ordinary conjuror! I went up in a balloon one day, quite near Kansas, Dorothy. The rope broke, and the balloon floated over this country. When it came down, the people thought I must be a Wizard, and made me their ruler!"

"But how did you work all those tricks?" asked Dorothy.

"I'll show you!" And he opened a cupboard full of models and masks. The Bald Head was a paper globe on a wire, with threads to move its eyes and mouth.

"How did you manage the voices?" she asked.

"I was a ventriloquist once!"

"So you're not a real Wizard at all!" said the Scarecrow. "And you can't keep those promises!"

"You're a very bad man!" said Dorothy severely.

"No, I'm quite a good man!" said the Wizard. "I'm just a very bad *Wizard*!"

THE MAGIC HUMBUG KEEPS HIS PROMISE

The Wizard promised to do his best for them, even though he wasn't a real wizard.

He opened up the Scarecrow's head, took out some straw, and put in some bran and some pins and needles.

"Now you've got brains!" he said, and the Scarecrow went away happy.

Then he cut a square out of the Tin Woodman's chest and put in a little red silk heart, stuffed with sawdust. He soldered the patch on again. "There! You've got a heart!" he said.

43

Next came the Lion. The Wizard gave him a drink from a green bottle.

"What's this?" asked the Lion.

"If you get it inside you, it will be courage. Courage always comes from inside! Courage is when you feel afraid, but you still do the brave thing!"

"I shall feel much braver now I *know* I have courage inside me!" said the Lion.

"It didn't need much magic to do that!" thought the Wizard. "They were already clever, kind and brave, but they didn't know it!"

But the Wizard was not so lucky in helping Dorothy. He decided to make another balloon out of strips of silk. The Tin Woodman lit a fire, and they filled the balloon with hot air. The Wizard fastened a clothes basket underneath it, got in, and called to Dorothy to hurry.

But she could not find Toto in time, and when she ran up, the balloon had gone up in the air without her! "Come back!" she cried.

"I can't!" called the Wizard. "Goodbye!"

And all the people waved and shouted "Goodbye!" as he mounted up into the clouds.

AWAY TO THE SOUTH

Dorothy's friends tried to comfort her. "Why don't you stay here with us in the Emerald City?" they suggested.

But Dorothy wanted to go back to her Aunt Em and Uncle Henry, in Kansas. "It may not be beautiful," said Dorothy, "but I would rather be there than anywhere else. There's no place like home!"

Then the Scarecrow had one of his ideas. "You still have the Golden Cap! Won't the Winged Monkeys help you? They could take you to the Good Witch of the South!"

So Dorothy called the Winged Monkeys. They came down out of the sky and carried them all to the foot of the ruby throne of the beautiful Good Witch of the South. Her name was Glinda, and she had rich red glowing hair, blue eyes, and a sparkling white dress.

"What can I do for you, my child?" she asked.

Dorothy told her story.

Glinda leaned forward and kissed her cheek. "I can tell you what to do," she said, "but first you must give me the Golden Cap."

"Here it is," said Dorothy.

"Now," said Glinda to the Scarecrow. "What are you going to do when Dorothy goes home?"

"The people of the Emerald City have asked me to be their ruler."

"And you?" she asked the Tin Woodman.

"The Winkies of the West want me to rule over them, since we killed the Witch."

"And what about the Lion?"

"The Beasts of the Forest have asked me to be their King!" said the Lion proudly.

"Then I shall command the Winged Monkeys to take each of you to your kingdoms. After that I shall give the King of the Monkeys the Golden Cap, so they will be free for ever."

"What about me?" said Dorothy.

"You have the silver slippers, my child. They are powerful magic, and all you have to do is to tell them where you want to go!"

"So I could have gone home the very first day I came here!"

"But then I wouldn't have got my brains!" said the Scarecrow.

"Nor I my heart!" said the Tin Woodman.

"Nor I my courage!" said the Lion.

"That's true!" said Dorothy. "I'm glad to have helped my friends. But now they are happy, I should like to go back to Kansas!" and she picked up Toto.

"Knock your heels together three times and tell the slippers where you want to go!" said Glinda.

"Take me home to Aunt Em!" said Dorothy. Instantly she was whirling through space so swiftly she could hear and see nothing. She rolled over on the grass several times before she knew where she was.

"Good gracious!" she cried.

For there was the Kansas prairie and in front of her was a brand new farmhouse, and Uncle Henry milking the cows.

The silver slippers had fallen off and disappeared.

Dorothy ran towards the house. Aunt Em was watering the cabbages. Toto followed, barking happily.

"My darling child!" Aunt Em said, hugging and kissing her. "Where did you come from?"

"From the Land of Oz!" said Dorothy. "And, Aunt Em, I'm so glad to be home again!"